All That Glitters

D1043816

All That Glitters

Written by Tisha Hamilton

SCHOLASTIC INC.
New York Toronto London Auckland Sydney
Mexico City New Delhi Hong Kong Buenos Aires

ISBN 0-439-75309-0

TROLLZ and its logo and all related characters TM & © 2005 DIC Entertainment, under license from DAM. All rights reserved.

Published by Scholastic Inc.
SCHOLASTIC and associated logos are trademarks and/or registered trademarks of Scholastic Inc.

12 11 10 9 8 7 6 5 4 3 2 1   5 6 7 8 9 10/0

Printed in the U.S.A.
First printing, October 2005

1

A Lucky Rainbow World

"Are we lucky, or what?" Amethyst Van Der Troll sighed, waving at the trees around her and her friends. It was the Time of the Great Tree Changing in Trollzopolis, one of the most beautiful times of the year. This was when the many tall trees that grew in Trollzopolis began to transtrollify, sprouting gorgeous showy blossoms from each branch. Amethyst and her four best friends — Topaz Trollhopper, Onyx Von Trollenberg, Ruby Trollman, and Sapphire Trollzawa — were on their way to school, marveling at the foliage.

"I'd rather be bald than live anywhere else," Sapphire agreed as she eyed a fantastic sky-blue flower with sparkling aqua tendrils. She was thinking about painting a similar flower on one of her blue sweaters. It would look so amazing, especially if she could get the shining colors just right.

"Trollzopolis is so styling, even the trees are getting into the act," Topaz added. This remark made Ruby stop walking. Her friends paused and looked back at her. She stood in the center of the walk, gazing up at the rainbow hues in the trees. "Styling," she muttered to herself. "Hmmm. I wonder."

The trees really were amazing this time of year. Normally, they all looked pretty similar: tall brown trunks, long brown branches, silky green leaves. But during the Changing they were all wildly different. Enormous, many-petaled flowers bloomed everywhere. Some were like flowers within flowers, with mounds of petals in glowing colors. Some were lacy with delicate curling tendrils. Still others took on elaborate shapes such as trumpets or flying birds. The branches were so heavy with spectacular blooms that they sometimes brushed the tops of the girls' heads as they walked.

Now Ruby had her eye on a particularly beautiful rosalea tree. Its flowers burst forth in swirling patterns of darker and lighter reds. The center of each deep red cluster of petals resembled a faceted jewel.

She reached up and plucked one perfect bloom, and then another, and another. "Here, hold this a minute," she asked Onyx as she handed Onyx her hand mirror.

For a minute Onyx looked as if she might say no. Of the five friends, she definitely had the least patience with Ruby's vanity.

"Puh-leeze, Onyx!" Ruby urged. "Be a friend. Hold it like this."

Smiling grimly, Onyx held the hand mirror so Ruby could adjust her hairdo.

"There," Ruby said at last. "Gelled!" She had skillfully incorporated the blossoms into her hairdo, pulling it off as only she could. The combination of the jewel-toned flowers and Ruby's own naturally red hair was stunning. She looked outrageous *and* fabulous.

"Oh, Ruby," Amethyst exclaimed. "Leave it to you to come up with such a trollific idea!" Sapphire and Topaz nodded enthusiastically.

Even Onyx had to admire her friend's daring and originality. "It does look fantastic," she admitted. "Just don't expect me to try it anytime soon." Everyone laughed at this. Onyx was dedicated to her minimalist style. She always looked super-cool, but in a more streamlined way than Ruby's flash-and-glitter approach.

Amethyst regarded her friends affectionately. Really, they were all so different it was almost hard to understand how they stayed so close. But different as each was from the other, they all brought something special to their fivesome. That's why they were the BFFL — *Best Friends For Life*.

Today Onyx wore slim black pants under a black zigzag patterned poncho, and amazing boots made of fabric patchwork. Her dark hair was super curly, and she wore it in huge, funky pigtails. *Funny*, Amethyst mused to herself. *Onyx is really anti-fashion, and yet she always seems to look so cutting edge.*

Ruby was another story. Fashion was her passion. Amethyst didn't think she'd ever seen her friend wear the same outfit twice. Or if Ruby did wear an outfit again, she accessorized it so skillfully you couldn't tell. If fashion was her first love, then accessories had to be her second. And to Ruby, just about everything was an accessory, as she'd proved by swiping the flowers for her do.

If Ruby and Onyx were opposites, then Topaz was somewhere in the middle of the spectrum. With her golden hair and nonstop smile, Topaz was nice inside and out. She could be counted on always to look on the bright side of things, and she didn't have a mean bone in her whole body. True, she was sometimes a bit of a daydreamer, but her friends all knew that her heart was always in the right place. Her honest approach to things had helped the group out of some tight spots in the past.

I'm lucky in more ways than one, Amethyst thought. *Not only do I live in styling Trollzopolis, but I have the best friends ever. Real true-blue friends.* Involuntarily her eyes flicked toward Sapphire. Talk about true-blue!

Sapphire was the steadiest troll in the group. And from her blue hair and eyes to the blue clothes she favored, she was certainly the truest and bluest of the five friends. Whenever brains were needed, it was Sapphire who came to the rescue. She was a natural problem solver who could think her way out of almost any situation. Amethyst didn't know what they'd do without her sometimes.

As her friends' bright chatter swirled around her, Amethyst smiled to herself. *I wonder how my friends would describe me*, she pondered.

"You're awfully quiet, Amethyst," Ruby pointed out. "You must have it bad for whoever it is if he's got you that distracted."

"No," Amethyst insisted, a faint blush creeping into her cheeks. "It's not a guy I'm thinking about."

"You know," Sapphire said seriously, "that color on your face goes great with your pink hair."

Everyone giggled.

"I was just thinking about how great you guys are and how you always make me laugh," Amethyst said. This wasn't exactly true, but it wasn't exactly a fib, either.

"Hear, hear," Topaz chimed in as the girls arrived at school. They headed inside to start the day.

2
The Great Changing Project

"Why, Ruby," Mr. Trollheimer greeted her. "That's . . . um, ahem . . . a um, very . . . ahem . . . unusual hairdo you've created there."

Ruby frowned for a second. She did not exactly consider the word "unusual" a compliment. Still, this *was* Mr. Trollheimer talking. He was hardly known for his fashion-forward thinking. In fact, the more Ruby thought about it, the more she thought that an outright compliment from Mr. Trollheimer was really *more* cause for worry. And Mr. Trollheimer was also her teacher, so it was probably a good idea to stay on his pleasant side. She quickly replaced the frown with a sweet smile and batted her red eyelashes. "Thank you, Mr. Trollheimer," she said politely before taking her seat. Then she turned and gave a half-resigned, half-humorous look to her four friends, who sat behind her and on either side.

Amethyst and Topaz smiled sympathetically. Onyx simply raised her eyebrows as if to say, "What did you expect?" Sapphire pursed her lips. When she was in school, Sapphire was all business. She didn't have time for anything that wasn't directly related to class work.

I guess that's probably why she always makes the Trollz Honor Roll and I don't, Ruby thought a little glumly. Then she brightened. After all, sometimes a troll had to make a choice: head of the class — or head of the fashion police. And when it came right down to it, Ruby had to admit she'd pick fashion over school-work any day. A droning noise began to penetrate her reverie. It was Mr. Trollheimer, but what was he talking about?

"And I can't think of a better time to do this than right now during the Great Changing," he was saying when Ruby tuned in. "Can anyone tell me what defines the five facets? What is it they all have in common? What is it that makes them facets?"

As usual, Sapphire's hand shot up first. "Yes, Sapphire?" Mr. Trollheimer called on her.

"Each of the five facets is a tree genus which is descended from the original five trees that formed the first Trollz habitat," she explained.

Ruby gaped at Sapphire while Mr. Trollheimer beamed. "Exactly!" he said. "I knew I could count on you, Sapphire."

How in Trollzopolis does she know that? Ruby wondered. She'd never even heard of the five facets before. They sounded cool, though. Ruby wondered if they were sparkly, like faceted gemstones. If so, she didn't think she'd mind this project at all. She loved jewelry and began to imagine a fabulous tiara adorned with five huge gemstones in all the colors of the rainbow. That would look so fantastic in her shiny red hair! She'd be the queen fashionista of Trollzopolis for sure.

Mr. Trollheimer clapped his hands and Ruby snapped to attention again. "Okay, class, break into groups and discuss how you're planning to complete the project," he went on. "I'll expect your reports next week."

Ruby quickly joined her BFFL. "What project?" she whispered frantically. Onyx sighed, and Sapphire rolled her eyes. "Ruby, do you, like, *ever* pay attention in class?" she chided.

"Of course I do!" Ruby replied indignantly. "How would I even know there *was* a project if I hadn't been listening?"

"Oh, Ruby, Sapphire was just kidding," Amethyst said soothingly. Sapphire shot her a surprised look, but Ruby looked mollified. Amethyst hurried on. "The important thing for us to do right now is figure out how we're, uh, going to figure this out," Amethyst said.

"Well," Ruby said smoothly. "I think the first thing is to just set up our outline of the project. You know, state the objective and how we're going to accomplish it."

"That is so smart, Ruby," Topaz said admiringly.

Amethyst was amused to see Ruby preen at this remark, even though she was sure Ruby had suggested the outline to cover up the fact that she still didn't really know what the project was. From the skeptical look on Onyx's face it was clear she suspected the same thing.

"Sapphire, you're really organized," Amethyst began.

"I know, I know," Sapphire interrupted. "You want me to take our group's notes, right?" Although she seemed exasperated by the fact that her friends were relying on her for the notes, truthfully, she wouldn't have it any other way. Without waiting for an answer she pulled out a bright blue marker and a butterfly-shaped pad of blue lined paper. At the top of the page she now wrote the word "Objective" in block letters. "Collect one Changing blossom from at least four different trees representing four of the five facets. Collect a blossom from a tree in the fifth facet for extra credit. How does that sound?" Sapphire asked. Everyone nodded and she wrote it down.

"I just wish he'd tell us what the facets are," Topaz complained. "How will we figure that out on our own?"

"I know," Amethyst agreed. "That's the real kicker in this assignment."

"Well, the rosalea is definitely one of them," Onyx pointed out.

"How do you know that?" Topaz gasped.

"Well, first of all, it was seeing the rosalea flowers in Ruby's hair that made Mr. Trollheimer think of it," Onyx said, holding up one finger.

"Really?" Ruby wanted to know. "How do you know that?"

"Anyone who was *really* listening could tell you," Onyx said, exasperated. "He said so himself!"

"Ha, I *knew* that," Ruby claimed. "I just wanted to hear *you* say it, too."

"Yeah, right," Onyx muttered. "Whatever. And anyway, Obsidian once told me that the rosalea tree is very important to Trollzopolis. Plus its flowers are the purest of the reds, and rosalea is an important ingredient in many potions."

Obsidian was the mysterious owner of the Spell Shack in the mall, and the girls believed she might be one of the Ancients — the keepers of the original trollz magic.

"Onyx is right." Sapphire nodded. "Blumeria is another. I remember my mom telling me that a long time ago, because its color matches my hair."

"That's great!" Amethyst exclaimed. "Here I was so worried about how we'd figure out the facets, and we have half of them already."

"Half only if you don't count the extra credit for the fifth facet," Sapphire reminded her. "I'm definitely planning on our group getting all five."

"Oh, we'll get all five," Ruby said confidently. "Five

facets, five BFFL. Let's face it, we're unbeatable to the fifth power."

Everyone smiled at that. Before returning to their seats, they agreed to meet after school at Fizzy's Amber Caves Café to work out their collection plan. They could hardly wait to get started.

3

Easy as One, Two, Three

Fizzy's was at the mall, but that was pretty much it as far as its mall relationship went. The mall was bright and busy. Stepping into the amber cave that was Fizzy's was like stepping into another world that was dim and unhurried. Light filtering through its amber walls gave its atmosphere a golden glow, like thick honey with a light shining through it. Not that anyone could hold on to the honey image for long once they'd met the owner, Fizzy.

Just like his place, Fizzy was almost the complete opposite of the mall. He was crabby, slow, and especially impatient with anyone below the age of ninety-five. This is why it was so ironic that his place was *the* hangout of choice for all the teen trollz in Trollzopolis.

School let out at three o'clock, and thanks to the brilliant hover technology of skoots, the BFFL were able to saunter into Fizzy's by 3:15. Only Ruby seemed a little disappointed to find that their group was the first to arrive.

"Hey, the corner table's free," Amethyst pointed out. This coveted spot had many advantages. Since it was in the corner, it had more privacy than the other tables. More importantly, it provided a perfect spot to scope out anyone else coming into Fizzy's.

The girls were just taking their seats when a barking voice startled them.

"You girls ready to order?" the voice said. "This is a place of business, you know, so if you want to sit at a table, you're gonna have to order something."

Fizzy's shaggy head and skinny, bent torso appeared from behind the long counter that ran along one wall.

"You'd think by now we'd be used to Fizzy," Onyx muttered. "But when he sneaks up on us like that, it just totally frizzes me out."

"Of course we're going to order something, Fizzy," Ruby said smoothly. "Just give us two minutes to make up our minds, okay?" She gave him a big smile, and he grunted and bent below the counter again.

The trollz studied the sparse menu, not that there was really much point to this activity. They almost always ordered the exact same thing, and by now Fizzy should have had it completely memorized. Five trollburgers, five orders of trolliez, extra ketchup, and a round of Trizzies. Ruby sauntered over to the counter.

"We're ready," she sang out. This was followed by a crash and an agonized cry as Fizzy again emerged from beneath the counter, this time rubbing his head. "What?" he grumbled. "Whaddaya want now?"

"Oh, I'm sorry," Ruby said sweetly. "Did I startle you?" She turned and winked at her friends in the corner. "We just didn't want to keep you waiting." She gave him their order and returned to the table.

"What's up, t-rollz?" Rock Trollhammer shouted as he walked in the door. The rest of his posse — cute Coal Trollwell, moody Flint Trollentino, hip-hop hottie Jasper Trollhoun, and Trollzopolis's youngest tycoon, Alabaster Trollington III — followed him.

"Hey, guys," Topaz called back. The guys settled in at the next table, and they all immediately began comparing notes on the big project. At first the girls held back a little; they didn't want to give away the fact that they'd already figured out two of the facets. Then super-jock Rock let them in on the third.

Amethyst nearly fell off her chair. Rock was known for his brawn, *not* his brains, but here he was, earnestly offering information about the vitronic tree.

"Well, like, vitronic is a kind of miracle cure tree," he explained. "If you boil the leaves, it makes a multi-vitamin herbal tea that helps fight off illness," he said, flexing his huge arm muscles.

"How do you think I keep so healthy during the football, wrestling, *and* track and field seasons? Like, the tea helps feed my body's building blocks."

"But are you sure it's a facet?" Topaz wanted to know.

"Well, it makes sense that it would be," Sapphire said thoughtfully. "Vitronic is the only known source of all the essential trollz nutrients, so that would make it an essential tree, so it's only logical that it would be . . ."

"One of the five facets!" Ruby exclaimed. "So now we have three: rosalea, blumeria, and vitronic."

"Now *that's* creative synergy," Alabaster put in.

"You had two, we gave you one, and now we all have three."

"That calls for a toast," Jasper announced. "Fizzy, my man. We need another pitcher of Trizzies right away!"

"You kids are always askin' me for stuff," Fizzy complained as he started pouring.

The girls looked at each other and giggled. There was just no pleasing Fizzy. Either he was mad because you weren't ordering, or he was annoyed because you were. When their new drinks arrived, Amethyst nodded meaningfully at each of her friends. This was a special code they'd worked out. Whenever one of the BFFL used it, it meant she had something to tell the others — in private. They finished their drinks and got ready to leave. As they headed out they heard Flint muttering as he scribbled in his ever-present journal. "Vitronic, it's atomic, it's a sweet troll tonic," he said thoughtfully. "My muse is with me. This poem is going to be great!"

"I'll believe that when I see it," Amethyst told her friends, and they all laughed. Once they got outside, though, they were instantly serious.

"What is it, Am?" Topaz asked.

"I think I figured out the fourth facet," Amethyst told them excitedly.

"So why couldn't you tell us that inside?" Ruby wanted to know.

"Well, explaining about the fourth facet would reveal how we're going to find them, and I just didn't think that was something we wanted to blab all over the place."

Sapphire looked worried. "I have a feeling I know where you're going with this, Am, and I don't like it one little bit," she said.

"But, Sapph, don't you see?" Amethyst argued. "It's the only way."

"Uh-oh," Onyx said as she realized what Amethyst meant.

"Hello? You're breaking up!" Topaz shouted in frustration. "Would someone please explain what you're all talking about?"

"The thing is," Amethyst began, "I'm pretty sure the fourth facet is ebonthorn, and the only place *I* know it grows is . . ."

"Just outside the Haunted Woods," Onyx finished.

The Haunted Woods was scary, and not exactly a fun place to hang out. Every troll grew up hearing the spooky stories, and the Haunted Woods was where every troll nightmare came from. It was a dark, forbidding place full of creepy-crawlies, and even worse things the trollz could hardly begin to imagine.

"You're right, though, Am," Sapphire told her. "It makes perfect sense that ebonthorn is the fourth facet. How many charms are carved from ebonthorn? Practically all of them," she went on. "That tells you how important it is. Plus it's the only tree with black leaves, and I'm beginning to figure out that the one thing that's the same about all the facets is that each is unique. They all have some feature that sets them apart from the other trees."

"We don't have to go *into* the forest," Amethyst hurried on, eager to convince her friends. "We could just stay on the edge. If we do it together, nothing can happen to us. Plus it's the ultimate tree habitat, and the only place where you can find all four of the facets we've identified growing in one place. It'll make finishing the project so much easier."

Reluctant as they each felt about going near the

Haunted Woods, Amethyst's friends had to agree with her. They decided to meet the next day right after school and ride their skoots together to the edge of the woods. They just hoped they'd return as carefree as they felt right now.

4

The Haunted Woods

"Okay, first we need to agree on a few rules," Sapphire said the next day as they stood near the edge of the Haunted Woods. Each troll carried a special expandable mesh tote bag that would help her collect and preserve her specimens. Trees grew thickly all around them here at the edge of the forest, but nowhere near as thickly as in the woods proper.

"One: whoever finds a facet tree agrees to collect five blossoms, one for each of the BFFL," Amethyst suggested.

"Good." Topaz nodded. "And how about two: we agree to try to keep in sight of each other, since this *is* the Haunted Woods?"

"Uh-huh," Onyx agreed. "And three: we all need to be super-careful not to go any farther into the forest than the very edge."

"Onyx is right," Sapphire warned. "Once you step inside these trees, there's no telling what can happen."

Ruby shivered. "Don't worry, I'm not going any farther than I have to," she said. "I wish there was some other way, but this is definitely the easiest. Let's each take a different direction and maximize our search area." With that, the girls cautiously set out.

Ruby just sauntered about looking for the coolest flowers. She was counting on her friends to tell her if she'd been lucky enough to snag one — or more! — of the facets. And if she hadn't, well, she figured she could always use the flowers for some styling accessories.

She saw one, then another, and another perfect flower. Soon her bag was stuffed with fabulous blossoms. That's when a rosy gleam shone from under a nearby tree. Ruby blinked and looked again. She *wasn't* imagining things: a flicker of ruby-red light winked at her from the base of a large tree. Ruby hurried forward to investigate. She didn't realize it, but she was now deep in the Haunted Woods.

When she arrived at the spot, what she saw nearly took her breath away. "Oh, trollipop!" she whispered. It was the most stunning red gem she'd ever seen. *Wow!* she thought, her eyes growing larger and larger as she stared into the stone. Its beauty was almost hypnotic. Suddenly she shook her head. What time was it anyway? She turned to head back to find her friends. She could hardly wait to show the BFFL what she had discovered. Quickly, she snatched the gem from the ground and stuffed it in her pocket. Then she hustled out of the forest.

Meanwhile, true to her nature, Sapphire had taken a very methodical approach to finding her facets. She had downloaded a list of the optimum growth conditions for each of the facets: what type of soil it grew best in, whether it flourished in sun or shade, and how tall it grew. Armed with this information, she'd started her search in the most likely place, heading toward the southern end of the forest's border.

A funny thing happened, though. Every time Sapphire saw a blossom she thought was perfect for the project, she'd soon spy another just a little farther away. Since she was trying to get five perfect specimens, she'd go after that one, too. Without realizing it, she was venturing deeper and deeper into the Haunted Woods with each step. Finally, she had her fifth fantastic blumeria blossom. Carefully, she clutched her bag and turned to head back to join her friends.

Then something caught her eye. It was beautiful and sparkling, and it was the same color as Sapphire's hair — a deep, penetrating blue. Quickly she raced toward the gleaming spot. When she reached it, she could hardly believe her eyes. There, lying on the ground, was the most awesome blue gemstone she had ever seen. Talk about facets! It must have had a million of them, and as the sun shone through the leaves of the forest's canopy, the gem glittered and glowed as if it burned with a blue-hot flame.

Wait 'til I show the BFFL, Sapphire thought. Little did she know it, but as she hurried out of the forest, her friends were all doing the same thing. Like Ruby and Sapphire, each had wandered a little farther into the forest than she'd meant to. Each had found a spectacular gem that matched the color of her hair. Their collection mission forgotten in their excitement, each was hurrying back to the meeting place eager to show her friends what she'd found.

For Amethyst, the gem's pink glow had beckoned to her from the base of the first tree she'd approached.

Perhaps it was because she had been named for a pink gem that the color had always held a special fascination for Amethyst. Or maybe it was because the color was so comfortably familiar to her — after all, it wasn't only the color of her hair, but also that of most of her possessions! She'd found herself almost powerless to resist the pink glow as it pulled her closer and closer. Then, when she'd realized the glow came from a fabulous deep-pink gem nearly the size of her fist, Amethyst couldn't help reaching out to touch it. Once she'd touched it, of course, she just had to pick it up, and once she felt its strange warmth tickling her fingers, she found herself unable to let it go. *I have to show this to my friends*, she thought as she headed toward the meeting place.

When Topaz found her gem, it was a similar story. She, too, had tried her best to stay out of the woods. Gingerly searching at the edge of the tree line, she'd been lured farther in by a golden light that seemed to be blinking a signal at her. She'd catch sight of it and head toward it, only to find, frustratingly, that she'd lost it. Then she'd see it flare up just a little farther away than she'd first thought it had been. Soon she was determined to find the source of the beguiling golden gleam, and she focused all her energy on stalking it. When she finally reached it, she nearly cried with relief.

True to her name, Topaz had her share of golden gems, but she'd never seen anything like this one before. It glowed like molten metal, flashing and sparkling in a tonal rainbow of golden hues. Entranced, Topaz folded her hand around it and marveled at its perfection. She couldn't wait to share her incredibly lucky find with her friends.

Just as Onyx was a little different from all her friends, so was her experience finding her own special stone. She'd found an ebonthorn tree, but for some reason it wasn't in full bloom. Instead of showy flowers, it was dotted with tightly furled buds. Onyx wondered about this. Was it possible, she asked herself, that the Great Changing happened at a different time in the woods than it did in town? She gathered a few of the buds anyway. Maybe they'd open if she put them in water.

Being in the Haunted Woods made Onyx feel a little nervous, but something about this ebonthorn was very soothing. Onyx had felt better as soon as she'd caught sight of it. She decided to rest a little before continuing her flower-gathering mission. Dreamily, she sank to the ground with her back against the trunk. "Mmmmm," she murmured. Onyx always felt at peace in nature, and now the warmth at the heart of this living tree seemed to seep into her back as she rested. Soft moss at its base formed a springy green cushion. Onyx sighed as she pressed her fingers into its feathery softness.

Then Onyx had felt something unusual. Its sharply angled sides felt smooth and strangely vibrant, almost as if something hummed deep inside. Onyx scrabbled to get hold of it, wondering if it might be a natural crystal formation. It would be unusual to find one lying in a patch of moss, for natural crystals were much more likely to be found in a cave surrounded by other formations. But what else could it be?

Once she'd tugged the gem free and taken a good look at it, she could hardly believe her eyes. Its chiseled facets reflected more light than Onyx would have thought possible in the dim environs of the woods. The gem was purely opaque and the deepest purple Onyx had ever seen. It was so dark, the gem was almost black, and it also seemed to glow from within. Onyx could feel its energy as she curled her fingers around it. *The BFFL have to see this to believe it,* Onyx thought fiercely.

Now they'll understand why dark colors are so beautiful to me.

So it came to be that all five BFFL were hurrying toward their meeting place. Each clutched an enchantingly exquisite gem that she couldn't wait to show the others. Except for Sapphire, each seemed to have completely forgotten her original purpose in going into the woods. And now, even though Sapphire had gathered her blossoms, she, too, was focused on only one thing: the bewitching gem in her pocket.

5

Secrets Among Friends

When Sapphire skidded into the clearing, she was surprised to find everyone there ahead of her. They stood around, looking oddly awkward.

"Oh," Sapphire gulped. "Hey, what are you guys doing? Am I, uh, late?"

"Oh, no, no," Amethyst assured her.

"Us?" Topaz added. "We're not doing anything. Just waiting . . ."

"Yeah, for you, trollipop!" Ruby said sunnily. Of the five, she alone seemed completely untroubled.

A weird thing had happened. Even though each of the girls couldn't wait to show off her lucky find, once she arrived at the meeting place, she felt strangely reluctant to share her gem. The only person this didn't bother was Ruby. *They'll all see it soon enough,* she reasoned. *Just as soon as I figure out the best way to show it off.*

"Want to see what I found?" Sapphire blurted. Her friends' heads swiveled in her direction like clockwork.

"What?" they all asked at once. Then they stopped and looked at each other in consternation.

"That was weird," Amethyst volunteered.

"Yeah, but what did Sapphire find?" Topaz added in a hurry.

Sapphire reached into her bag, aware of her friends' eyes fastened on her. Was it her imagination or did they all seem to heave a sigh when all she pulled out were the five perfect blumeria flowers?

"Those are gorgeous," Onyx gasped. "And you found five! Oh, Sapphire, you're the best!"

Sapphire wanted to show them her real find — the fascinating gem. But now that they were all together she found that she kept making up perfectly good reasons for keeping it under wraps for now. *What if one of them says she lost it?* Sapphire didn't think she could bear to part with it. Then she shook her head. What was she thinking? These were her best friends! They shared everything, right? *Still, there's something unusual about this stone,* Sapphire found herself thinking. *Maybe I'd better examine it at home before showing it off to anyone.*

"So, what did you guys find?" she asked brightly.

"Oh, nothing," Topaz said too quickly.

"Nothing?" Sapphire repeated in astonishment. "Did you forget about the project?"

"Oh, right," Onyx said. "The project."

This was so unlike Onyx, Sapphire didn't know what to think. Really, her friends were all acting *so* strange. Now Onyx was pulling a few ebonthorn specimens from her bag. She didn't have five, and the ones she did have were just tiny buds.

"I don't know," Onyx said slowly. "Maybe today wasn't a good day to do this."

"Yeah, the project isn't due until next week anyway," Amethyst added.

"I couldn't really find any good specimens," Topaz explained.

If Sapphire hadn't been feeling so peculiar herself, she would have called her friends on their uncharacteristic behavior. *Am I acting as weird as they are?* she asked herself. Still, Ruby's bag bulged with blossoms. At least someone other than Sapphire had tried to finish the project.

"Ruby, what's in your bag?" Sapphire pressed. "It looks like you found loads of specimens."

"Yeah, look!" Ruby said eagerly. She opened her bag and a riot of colorful blossoms spilled out. Each was perfect and each was beautiful, but none of them were facet blossoms.

"Ruby, did you forget that you were actually looking for something specific out there, or what?" Sapphire challenged.

"You know, I don't know," Ruby said thoughtfully. "I guess I just got so bedazzled by all these fabulous flowers, maybe I did forget. But hey, like Am says, we have days and days to finish this, right?"

"Exactly," Topaz agreed.

"Anyway, it's getting kind of late," Amethyst pointed out. "And I, uh, promised my mother I'd do something, so maybe we should all just go home. We can meet again tomorrow."

"Good idea," Ruby said quickly. "Let's just start fresh tomorrow. Same time, same plan. We'll skoot over right after school."

Onyx shivered. "I hate having to come here again," she confessed. "The Haunted Woods gives me major creeps."

"I don't think anyone likes the idea of being near the Haunted Woods," Topaz ventured.

"You've got that right," Sapphire said. "I just wish we'd finished the project today."

"Don't worry, Sapph." Amethyst tried to comfort her friend. "We'll get it done tomorrow for sure."

"After all, why work at something today when you can always put it off until tomorrow?" Ruby said, light-hearted as ever. The girls giggled uneasily in reply. Then they boarded their skoots and headed home, each anxious to look at her gem in the privacy of her own room.

6

Gem Obsessions

Amethyst raced upstairs as soon as she got home. She shut her bedroom door and flopped down on the mattress. She could hardly wait to pull the magnificent pink gem out of her pocket. *What is wrong with me?* she thought. Her hands were actually trembling as she cupped the vibrant stone. It was just so beautiful.

She felt only a little bad about not sharing her amazing find with her friends. She couldn't explain why, but she just felt she needed some time alone with it first. She wanted to enjoy it — revel in it even — all on her own. Somehow, that made the gem more special. After all, it had called out to *her*, hadn't it? She'd been hunting in the woods when it flashed its magical light at her. And of course it was pink, her favorite color.

"Amethyst!" her mother called. "It's time for dinner."

Amethyst blinked and looked at the clock on her bedside table. How could it be six o'clock already? She'd arrived home around five. Had she really been staring at the gem for a whole hour? Well, it *was* incredibly beautiful to look at, with its twinkling inner depths. She stuck it under her pillow and headed downstairs. Midway down, she stopped and ran back to her room. This time, she grabbed the gem and stuck it in her pocket. Then she headed back downstairs for dinner.

Amethyst didn't know it, but a similar scene was taking place at each of her friends' houses. Onyx found her shining deep purple gem so hypnotic she could hardly take her eyes off it. It just made her feel so peaceful and happy. Whenever she did manage to tear her eyes away from it, she felt vaguely troubled. There was some power in this stone that Onyx didn't understand, but she could tell by the way she felt in its presence that it was something special, and something just for her. She hadn't liked keeping it from her friends, but now she felt sure that had been the right decision.

With an effort, she left the gem on her desk while she rustled under her bed. There it was! Onyx pulled out an elaborate necklace made of shining dark stones. She'd bought it at the mall and it had only cost a few trollars, so she knew the stones were plain colored glass. Working carefully, she pried several of the central stones loose. Then she replaced them with the single gem she'd found in the forest. There! No one would notice it in the middle of so many similar stones. Now Onyx could keep it close and hidden at the same time.

The same thing was happening with Topaz, too. She'd spent a long time mesmerized by her new golden gem. Like the others, she wanted to keep it close to her, but she also wanted to keep it secret. Now Topaz did something that would have been unthinkable to her before she found the stone. She took the special ring, that had come from her great-grandmother, and she flipped its secret lever. The lever opened the back of the ring so its topaz gem could be removed. Topaz gently removed the original stone and replaced it with the one she'd found in the woods. Only someone looking very closely would ever notice the difference — and Topaz planned to make sure no one got that close. This way she could keep the stone on her, and look at it anytime she wanted, without anyone else knowing. For some reason, the idea of keeping her newfound gem secret was very important to Topaz.

Over at the Trollzawa house, Sapphire grappled

with her own problems. On her way home from the forest, she'd decided to take a scientific approach to the stone. First she would examine it under her trollescope. Then she planned to use her chemistry kit to perform a few harmless tests. She knew her stone was a sapphire, but there was definitely something unusual about it and Sapphire was determined to figure out what it was.

When she got home, though, it was hard to concentrate on her experiments. Trying to view it under the trollescope only enlarged the gem's sparkles and made Sapphire feel a little sunblind. She tried adjusting the enlargement and the angle at which she was looking at the stone, but each time the same thing happened.

"It's almost like you're fighting me," she actually said out loud. Then she clapped a hand to her forehead and whispered, "Am I losing my mind or what? Help! I'm talking to a stone!"

Sapphire knew there was something a little unhealthy about the stone. She felt dishonest for having kept it a secret from everyone. And yet every time she made up her mind to tell someone about it, she found herself changing her mind at the last minute. She thought about how oddly her friends had acted when they'd all met up after they'd been out collecting. Was it her imagination or had they all seemed kind of nervous, especially when she'd asked them what they'd found. Sapphire had meant to tell them then about her stone, but instead she had told them about the blumeria blossoms. What if they'd found stones, too, and then didn't want to tell anyone about them?

Sapphire shook her head. *That's crazy,* she told herself. *And unlikely,* she added. It would be too much of a coincidence if they'd each found a special gem in the forest. Wouldn't it?

With considerable effort, Sapphire resolutely decided to stop thinking about the stone. She rummaged in her bedside table drawer and finally pulled out a small, carved box. It was made of shiny black obsidian and had a small sapphire set in its top. It had been a gift from her grandmother when she had been just a tiny troll. Young as she was at the time, though, Sapphire could still remember what her grandmother had told her about the box. "I've embedded this with a special safety spell," she had said. "It will always keep you — and anything you put inside it — safe."

The stone fit perfectly, and Sapphire's grandmother must have been right. As soon as the box was shut, Sapphire stopped worrying about the stone. In fact, she felt a whole lot better. After dinner with her family, she finished up her homework and went to bed with a smile on her face. Since she'd put it in the obsidian box, Sapphire hadn't felt like looking at the stone once.

Ruby was also smiling when she slid under the covers that night. She'd experimented with her blossoms for hours, styling and restyling her hair until she'd created the most marvelous new hairdo using some of the best flowers she'd collected. Topping it all off, of course, would be her special red gem. She could hardly wait to show it off at school the next day. She'd carefully placed the flowers she planned to use in water so they'd be fresh and ready for her hair in the morning. As she turned off the light, her red gem seemed to wink at her from her night table.

Ruby's Fib

Sapphire woke up the next day refreshed and reenergized. Before she left for school, she tucked the obsidian box inside her pocket. She felt a lot less worried about the mystical stone today, but she still wanted to make sure nothing happened to it. If she kept it in her pocket she'd know exactly where it was at all times. And until she figured out what was going on with the stone, she figured that was for the best.

Amethyst had finally decided to keep her stone in a little filigree box that hung from her spells bead bracelet. The box was really for holding spell and amber beads, but the stone fit perfectly. No one could see it, but Amethyst knew it was there and she could open the box to take a look at the stone whenever she wanted to.

Topaz wore her ring, and Onyx wore her necklace. Amethyst had her bracelet, and Sapphire fingered the box in her pocket. When they met up at school that morning they were all hiding something from each other. Everyone but Ruby, that is.

When she sauntered up, the other trollz gasped. She had worked some truly stunning-looking rainbow-colored flowers into her hairdo again, but this time a brilliant red gem also gleamed from the center of her do.

"Ruby!" Sapphire managed to squeak. "Your hair looks fantastic with those amazing flowers in it. And where did you get that gorgeous gem?" Sapphire tried to act casual, but she was paying very close attention.

Now she knew it wasn't her imagination. The other trollz seemed just as interested in hearing Ruby's answer as she was. Sapphire felt certain that they all knew more about the mysterious gem than they were revealing. Just like she did.

"This old thing?" Ruby said with a laugh. "It's been in my family for trolleons. Can you believe it? I found it in an old box in the basement. This cool thing was just tossed in there with a bunch of junk like old trinkets and stuff. It's a good thing I rescued it. It could have been thrown away by mistake."

Sapphire watched as Amethyst, Topaz, and Onyx blinked with surprise at this answer. *A-ha*, she thought. *They seem surprised because they were expecting to hear something else.* The fact that she and all her friends were hiding something was bothersome for Sapphire, but not nearly as upsetting as the thought that Ruby might be telling an outright lie.

Or was she? Really, when she looked at it logically, the chance of such a coincidence seemed nearly impossible. *Oh, Sapphire, wake up and smell the swamp gas,* she told herself firmly. *You must be imagining things. The BFFL do* not *hide things from each other, and they certainly don't lie.*

Sapphire pushed aside the nagging thought that, at least as far as she was concerned, this wasn't really true. She wasn't really hiding anything from her friends, she told herself, she was just waiting for the right moment to tell them about her find.

Ruby, meanwhile, was having second thoughts of her own. She hadn't meant to tell such a whopper — and to her BFFLs! But it had just popped out. The more she pondered it, the more convinced she became that it was really for the best. *After all,* she reasoned to herself, what does it really matter where I found it? The point is it's mine — and it does look fabulous in my hair. It goes so perfectly with my natural coloring that I'm the only one who could do it justice, anyway. She shrugged away her worries.

Then the bell rang. Maybe Ruby would tell her friends the truth later on, when they got together again to finish their project.

Try, Try Again

After school that day, the five trollz met outside the Haunted Woods again. Everyone seemed a little nervous, even the usually carefree Ruby. She was fidgeting and kept shifting her weight from one foot to the other.

"I don't know what happened last time, but this time let's try to stick to the program, okay?" Sapphire begged her friends.

"What do you mean?" Ruby snapped. "I didn't come back empty-handed."

"Yeah, well, you didn't come back with anything that helped us finish the project, either," Sapphire shot back.

The other three looked shocked. The BFFL rarely fought with each other. Something strange was definitely in the air.

"It's no wonder we're all in a frizzy, with the Haunted Woods looming over us," Amethyst said soothingly. "But let's not bicker or blame each other, okay? I was the biggest loser of all yesterday, but I'm going to make up for it today."

"You know, Sapphire, you already found all the blumeria we need," Onyx pointed out. "Maybe you should just go home."

"And leave my BFFL by the Haunted Woods? No way, t-rollz," Sapphire insisted. "Anyway, maybe I'll get lucky and find the fifth facet." *And maybe I'll get lucky and find another gemstone*, she thought. If only she knew that each of her friends was thinking the exact same thing.

Once again the girls started searching on the edge of the woods, but soon found themselves inching closer and closer to the Haunted Woods. In fact, as soon as they were out of sight of the others, the first thing Amethyst, Onyx, Topaz, and Sapphire all did was to take out their gemstones to look at them. Ruby used her hand mirror to admire how her gem brought out the lively color of her red hair. It even picked up rainbow tints from the exotic flowers she'd found.

"It's so beautiful," Ruby crooned as her gem seemed

to catch a glint of light from somewhere and began glowing. The glint seemed to be coming from somewhere in the Haunted Woods, but where? Ruby leaned forward. What was that gleam she spied just beyond that tree? She just *had* to investigate.

Meanwhile, Sapphire was admiring her own gem when she thought she saw something sparkling in the forest just beyond the trees. Was there another gem in there? *I'd better check it out*, she thought. But whenever she got close to the place she thought she'd seen it, the glinting light was always just a little farther away. *That's funny*, she thought as she continued to move deeper and deeper into the woods.

Amethyst was tracking her own mysterious winking light when she noticed a wind begin to spring up around her. She pulled her sweater around her and tried to wait it out, but the wind only seemed to grow stronger. It almost felt as if it was pushing her in one direction. *Oh, well*, Amethyst thought, *I can't just stay here and fight it. It's too strong*. She, too, began moving deeper into the woods.

By the time Topaz and Onyx noticed the wind, they, too, were well into the forest. As it swirled around her, Onyx thought the rustling leaves sounded like someone laughing. The wind grew stronger and stronger until it was near hurricane strength.

Sapphire was struggling to see amid the swirling winds when she stumbled into a clearing. She quickly spotted Ruby because of the shining gem in her hair.

"Ruby!" Sapphire called out over the wind. "What's going on?"

"No idea!" Ruby shouted back. "It looks like a freak storm or something."

Sapphire and Ruby quickly realized that Amethyst, Topaz, and Onyx were in the clearing as well.

"Yeah, but what kind of storm would push us all toward one spot?" Onyx asked over the howling wind.

"Um, I think I know," Amethyst said, alarmed. "It feels like we're in some kind of tornado!"

All at once, the trollz screamed as the winds swirled more fiercely around them, lifting them off the ground. They clasped hands and squeezed their eyes shut against the gritty wind and the deafening noise.

Then just as suddenly as the wind had begun, it grew quieter. The trollz heard a high-pitched, childish laugh ring out in the air around them. Five pairs of eyes snapped open to see a shining pillar of white light spiraling up from the center of their circle. Then, to their horror, they saw wavering beams of light emanating from the gems in their bellybuttons. The beams met in the center of the white pillar and then . . . the gems went dark. Their powers were gone!

"Oh, my gosh!" Ruby gasped. "How did that happen?"

"What is going on?!" Sapphire shouted, panicked.

An evil cackle was their answer. "So many questions, my little trollkins, but you forgot the most important one," squealed a scratchy voice. "Who?"

A tiny green gremlin emerged from behind the glowing pillar. He looked no older than a nine-year-old boy, and his scowling green face was partially obscured by a blue baseball cap. Amethyst gasped. "It's Simon!" she said.

Simon was every troll's worst creepy nightmare. A twisted gremlin trapped in the body of an innocent-looking small boy, the girls forever regretted the awful mistake they'd made when they had accidentally freed Simon from his three thousand year "nap" in the Shadow World. They'd been tricked, first by Simon's nasty side-kick, the ogre-dog Snarf. Somehow he'd managed to persuade the girls that he was really a woman named Miss Tourmaline who could help them when their gems were beginning to dim.

Locked in "Miss Tourmaline's" shop, the girls had unwittingly fled straight into the Shadow World, a creepy place of ghostly shadows. That's where they'd found Simon, who'd fooled them by pretending to be a lost little boy. Thinking they were rescuing a child who'd accidentally fallen into the horrible, howling Shadow World, they'd taken him back through the portal to Trollzopolis with them. That's when they'd realized the truth about Simon. He wasn't a little boy at all, but rather a wicked gremlin bent on revenge and cruelty. They'd managed to defeat him that time, but now that he'd been freed from his Shadow World prison, he was always trying to trick his way back into Trollzopolis. He was desperate to avenge himself by destroying Trollzopolis and enslaving the trollz who lived there.

"That's right, my little trollkins," Simon said menacingly as he stepped closer. "I'm back."

9

Slaves of Simon

"Your powers are wasted on you," Simon gloated. "What can you trollz do? Little spells, that's all."

"Don't listen to him!" Amethyst urged her friends. "We know that's not true!"

"This mean little green thing is nothing but a nasty liar," Onyx added.

"Oh, ho, who's the liar?" Simon cackled. "Not me! It's true that separately your powers are rather ordinary, but together they add up to quite a lot. I'm not hiding anything! I'm very honest about what I want: to enslave you and the rest of Trollzopolis forever. *You're* the ones who aren't being honest."

"The gem," Sapphire whispered.

"What's that, little trolly?" Simon mocked. "Yes, you all have something you're hiding from each other, don't you? Oh, *excuuuuse* me. Ruby isn't hiding anything, but she's the only one."

"Of course not!" Ruby struggled to speak. "I don't hide things from my BFFL!"

"Of course not!" Simon mimicked meanly. "Instead of hiding something, you just chose to *lie* instead! I knew you weak little trollz wouldn't be able to resist the gems I left in the forest. You made it so easy to trap you. Greedy little trollz. You all had perfectly good power gems, but were you content? *Nooooooo!*"

Simon howled with glee. "All I had to do was leave a shiny bauble in your path and you were putty in my hands!"

"I wanted to tell you all about this sapphire I found," Sapphire admitted miserably. "But every time I tried, I just . . . didn't."

"Me, too!" cried Amethyst.

"I don't know why I told that stupid lie," Ruby confessed. "I didn't find my hair gem in the basement at all. I found it right here in the forest."

"I can't believe we all fell for the same trick," Onyx seethed. "All of a sudden everything we care about — each other and Trollzopolis — is at stake! And it's all because of some sparkly stones!"

"Oh, your pathetic little confessions are useless!" Simon chided them. "Your powers are gone, and so is your freedom. Soon all of Trollzopolis will be mine!"

"Maybe it's not too late," Topaz ventured. Her friends could see her fumbling with her ring. Soon she pulled the stone from its setting and held it cocked in her fist.

"On the count of three, right?" Amethyst asked as she took her stone from her bracelet.

"One!" Sapphire shouted as she felt for the box in her pocket. She worked the lid open and soon her stone was in her hand.

"Two!" hollered Onyx as she ripped the necklace from her throat.

The girls saw Ruby reaching for the gem in her hair, and Topaz called, "Three!"

Four shining stones flew through the air. Then they stopped, suspended on a thin red beam of light.

"The weakest link," Simon jeered. "Yes, I was counting on you, Ruby. Can't quite bring yourself to cast away that beautiful bling, can you?"

The beam that held the other stones was indeed emanating from Ruby's gem, which was still firmly in her hair. Frantically she scrabbled at it with her fingers, but it didn't seem to budge.

"Come on, Ruby," Amethyst urged. "Throw it away."

"Do it, Ruby," added Sapphire. "Do it now!"

"I-I can't," Ruby cried.

"Ruby, we'll go to the mall and get you another one," Topaz promised. "Just throw that one away, okay?"

"You don't understand," Ruby said through gritted teeth. "It's fighting me or something."

"Yes, it *is* fighting you," Simon sneered. "You're the weakest link. You don't have the strength to throw it away."

"Don't listen to him, Ruby," Onyx yelled. "He's lying. You can do it if you try."

"Aren't you trollz wondering why Ruby was the only one who actually *lied* about the stone?" Simon inquired.

"No!" the other girls shouted at him.

"Because she's the weakest link, the weakest link, the weakest link," Simon taunted.

Tears sprang to Ruby's eyes as she struggled with the gem. Simon was right. She *was* weak. Everyone else

had found the strength to give up their gems —
everyone except her. Her friends' lives were in danger,
and it was all her fault. Defeated, Ruby gave up and
stopped struggling. As her friends watched, aghast, as
her hands dropped to her sides and her eyes closed.

10
Friends to the Fifth Power

"Don't give up, Ruby," Amethyst called.

"Remember the BFFL," Onyx urged.

But Ruby made no sign that she'd heard. Her eerie stillness frightened her friends more than anything else that had happened so far.

"You're not alone," Topaz reminded her.

But there was still no response from Ruby.

"You said it yourself," Sapphire pointed out. "We're unbeatable to the fifth power — and that means you, too!"

Slowly Ruby's fingers began to flex. Her eyelids fluttered. Her friends could see that she was struggling to raise her arms, almost as if some invisible force was working against her to push them back down.

Simon cackled. "Kiss Trollzopolis — and your life

as you've known it — good-bye, little trollkins! You're in my power now!"

"You can do it, Ruby," her friends chanted. "We believe in you!"

Ruby strained against Simon's spell, and managed to get one hand around the gem in her hair. The other grabbed hold of one of the exotic blossoms that studded her do. Suddenly Ruby seemed to break free. Her eyes were wide open, her arms were moving naturally, and she looked like her old fighting self again.

Now Ruby used both hands, crushing the rainbow blossom she still clutched as she wrestled the gem from her hair. "Trollzopolis will never belong to you!" Ruby shouted. "Take that, Simon!"

Ruby hurled the red stone as hard as she could. It flew through the air. The crushed flower she'd also been holding followed at a somewhat slower pace, drifting through the air like a windblown leaf.

The ruby hung in the air a moment, suspended in the pillar of light around Simon along with the other four gems. Then the flower floated into the pillar. The light blazed brighter and brighter until, with a blinding flash, it exploded in a burst of rainbow-colored sparks.

"*Noooooooo!*" Simon wailed.

He seemed to have been sucked into a tornado all its own, spinning faster and faster in a dizzying downward spiral. With every spin he seemed to shrink a little. Finally, he was smaller than a soap bubble. A terrific cracking sound split the air. Simon howled with pain before vanishing into the ground in an enormous plume of black smoke.

11

The Fifth Facet

Once Simon had disappeared, the girls floated back to the ground. They were all a little dazed after their experience, and the lingering smoke stung their eyes. As the haze gradually cleared, they became aware of the gems.

Strangely, the five stones hadn't vanished with their evil master. But now, instead of the colored beams that had sparkled from each, there were only threads of fine white smoke. The white smoke seemed to shimmer for a moment, and it seemed to all five girls that a rainbow suddenly arced across the clearing. In the blink of a trollzeye it was gone. Only the glittering pile of gems remained.

"I'm sorry I let you down," Ruby apologized to her friends. Her chin trembled and tears threatened to spill down her face. She still felt terrible, and was surprised to see the rest of the BFFL all smiling at her.

"You didn't let us down," Amethyst pointed out.

"You saved the day, in fact," Onyx agreed.

"But I was the only one who couldn't throw away my gem. I almost destroyed Trollzopolis," Ruby wailed. "If it wasn't for you all coaching me, I couldn't have done it."

"But you *did* do it, Ruby," Topaz told her reassuringly. "That's all that matters now. You believed in us, and we believed in you. In the end, it was all of our bravery and strength that defeated Simon. We couldn't have done it without you!"

"And maybe something else, too," Sapphire added thoughtfully.

"What do you mean?" Amethyst asked.

"I've been thinking about those rainbow flowers in Ruby's hair," Sapphire mused.

"What about them?" Ruby wanted to know.

"Well, they're not like any other flower I've seen," Sapphire said. "All the others are mostly one color or another, like the way the blumeria is all different shades of blue or the rosalea is all different shades of red. The ones in Ruby's hair each have petals in every color of the rainbow."

"They *are* different," Onyx agreed thoughtfully.

"That makes them unique," Topaz added.

"Which means they might be the fifth facet," Sapphire suggested.

Ruby remembered how clutching the flower seemed to give her extra strength just when she needed it most.

"They are!" Ruby exclaimed. "I'm sure they are! I felt it when I was struggling with the gem."

"And I saw it when you tossed the flower into the circle of gems," Topaz said excitedly.

"Hey, maybe we can save Trollzopolis *and* finish the project for Mr. Trollheimer," Ruby giggled. Her friends were relieved to see that she was back to her old bouncy self.

"I'm sure I can find the tree I got these from," Ruby told her friends. "So why don't we make like a tree ourselves and *leave*!"

"I can't wait to get out of here," Amethyst agreed, laughing.

"What about the jewels?" Onyx wondered. The girls looked at them warily. They seemed harmless. The strange glinting lights that had seemed to come from the stones were gone. They were still beautiful, but the girls' unusual sense of their overpowering mystery had vanished with Simon.

"Let's take them to Obsidian," Sapphire suggested. "Whatever we do, I don't think we should just leave them here."

Cautiously, each girl retrieved her gem. As quickly as possible they made their way out of the Haunted Woods. As they reached the edge, Ruby gave a small cry.

"That's it," she announced. Then she pointed to a single tree in the group of more ordinary trees that ringed the edge of the Haunted Woods. It dripped with magnificent rainbow flowers.

Ruby carefully gathered five perfect samples. Sapphire held open one of the mesh collecting bags as Ruby gently laid them inside. Then the five trollz raced each other to their skoots and hopped on.

It was as though a dark cloud had been lifted from above their heads, and the farther they sped from the Haunted Woods, the better they felt.

12
Finders Keepers

When the girls arrived at Obsidian's place, they talked over each other in their eagerness to tell the story.

"And then I figured out . . ." Sapphire was saying.

"I tried to get rid of it . . ." Ruby was explaining.

"And then we noticed . . ." Topaz babbled.

"I still can't believe . . ." Onyx declared.

"Oh, Obsidian, it was just awful," Amethyst lamented.

Obsidian's ancient eyes twinkled as she held up one hand. Sparkling rings of shiny metal and glimmering gems shone from her fingers. Layer upon layer of silver and golden bracelets jingled on her wrist. The effect was that of a tiny tinkling bell. The girls quieted down at once.

"I can only listen to one of you at a time," Obsidian said kindly. "But first, let me pour you each a glass of trolltea. I can see you've all had quite an experience."

Trolltea was a famous herbal tea that had grown in Trollzopolis since the days of the Ancients. When it was brewed, it smelled wonderful, like a field of fresh flowers. As its soothing warmth slid down their throats, the girls found themselves feeling calm and completely free of the last vestiges of the fear that had gripped them during their ordeal.

Obsidian listened carefully as Amethyst, Sapphire, Onyx, Topaz, and last of all Ruby each told her story, beginning with the finding of her own gem and how it had made her feel. Then they took turns describing what had happened with Simon in the clearing.

"I'm very proud of you," Obsidian said when they were finished. "I know you all know it's not a good idea to venture into the Haunted Woods, but Simon's evil magic made sure you couldn't help yourselves."

Then she told them all about the auroriana tree. Sapphire had been correct in figuring out that the fifth facet was the auroriana tree. The blossoms that Ruby had blithely entwined in her hair were from the last of its kind in Trollzopolis.

Its rainbow-hued flowers were especially potent. All aspects of the tree — its leaves, wood, and flowers — were essential ingredients in spells to counteract evil magic. That's why Ruby had finally found her inner strength, and also why Simon's downfall had been so stunning and final.

"There's one more thing I need to tell you about the auroriana," Obsidian said, smiling broadly. "And then you need to get going and really finish that project for good this time."

The trollz waited expectantly. Obsidian gathered up the bright pile of gems they'd brought. She shook them gently in her hands and seemed to be intently listening.

"Ah, it's as I thought," she said. "I just had to make sure. Auroriana is a powerful antidote to any kind of evil, including enchanted stones. These gems are perfectly safe now, so go on and take them. They're yours."

"Really?" Ruby breathed.

"Really," Obsidian assured her. "Keeping them will help you remember the important lessons you learned today in the forest — lessons about truthfulness and friendship and standing up for what you know is right."

13

Top of the Class

"I can't believe it," Ruby said as they skooted to school the next day. "Trollzopolis is safe *and* I can still keep my totally gelled 'do."

Sure enough, Ruby was sporting her gem in her hair again. Her friends laughed.

"Hey," Ruby defended herself. "You can't keep a stylish troll down."

"Or her hair," Amethyst joked.

After they had left Obsidian's the previous day, they had made sure to finish their flower collection. This time, though, they stayed as far away from the Haunted Woods as possible. Onyx took the ebonthorn blossoms from a tree she'd never noticed before that was tucked away in a corner of her own backyard. Ruby took the rosalea blossoms from one of the trees they usually passed on their way to school. Topaz and Amethyst had persuaded Rock to tell them where to find the vitronic. They'd spent much of the evening t-mailing back and forth to complete their report. Today they'd be handing it in.

When they reached Mr. Trollheimer's classroom, he was very impressed. "Not only have you turned this in ahead of time, but you've completed it perfectly, including the extra credit," he praised them. "I'm very proud of you."

The five trollz took turns presenting their project to the class. Sapphire had created a terrific poster to display the blossoms. They'd all collaborated on the final report, but Ruby did most of the presenting, probably because she was the least self-conscious about standing up in front of the class and speaking. In the end, though, everyone pitched in, and each of the BFFL spoke about the particular facet she'd found.

When they were done, Mr. Trollheimer paid them a huge compliment. "I hope you were all paying attention," he told the class, "because this has been a great example of how a project should work." Then he gave the BFFL a conspiratorial wink. "You proved that friends really *can* work together and help each other out."

"I wonder what he meant by that," Onyx said later when they got together for lunch.

"He can't know anything about what happened in the Haunted Woods," Ruby asked with alarm. "I mean, can he?"

"I wonder," Sapphire said thoughtfully.

"Well, he had one thing right anyway," Amethyst declared. "The friends that stick together get the best grades on school projects."

"And the best hairdos," Topaz cracked.

"I think it calls for a celebration later," Ruby suggested. "Maybe . . ."

"Let me guess!" Onyx interrupted her. "At Fizzy's, right?"

"You know it, BFFL," Ruby agreed.

"Okay, but . . ." Sapphire put in.

"There's a 'but' to going to Fizzy's?" Topaz asked in surprise.

"Yeah, well," Sapphire stammered. "I just don't want any of us to lose sight of what we really learned doing this project."

"About telling each other the truth, you mean," Onyx added.

"And not keeping secrets," Sapphire finished.

"We're BFFL and that's set in amber," Ruby vowed. "That's what makes us special *and* gives us extra power. Don't worry, I won't ever forget that!"

Congratrollations!

You get 50 Trollars to spend on Trollz.com just for buying this book! After you've read the book go to Trollz.com and type in the code below to collect your 50 Trollars and have a chance to earn 300 more!

0-439-75309-01h2qw6299jq9

Create your own Trollz™ on TROLLZ.com

For more trollular fun check out
scholastic.com/trollz

You and your BFFL's (Best Friends For Life) **can**

- ☆ start your own Trollz™ Book Club
- ☆ print invites and bookmarks
- ☆ and get more cool stuff

Coming this Fall

Fun and fashion with a magical twist!

Available now wherever toys are sold!

Big Hair is Back!

Trollz
It's A Hair Thing!™

Create Your Own Trollz Online
TROLLZ.com

Meet the Trollz — five best friends who share everything together, including their newfound magic powers!
Hang out with the Trollz... they'll put a spell on you!